Look for these Just Right Books™

Just Right for 2's and 3's

HOW MANY KISSES GOOD NIGHT
By Jean Monrad/Illustrated by Eloise Wilkin

MINE! A SESAME STREET BOOK ABOUT SHARING
By Linda Hayward/Illustrated by Norman Gorbaty

THE NOISY COUNTING BOOK
By Susan Schade and Jon Buller

THE RAINY DAY PUDDLE
By Ei Nakabayashi

SALLY WANTS TO HELP
By Cindy Wheeler

SOUNDS MY FEET MAKE
By Arlene Blanchard/Illustrated by Vanessa Julian-Ottie

Just Right for 3's and 4's

THE JUST RIGHT MOTHER GOOSE
By Arnold Lobel

THE RUNAWAY CHRISTMAS TOY
By Linda Hayward/Illustrated by Ann Schweninger

SWEETIE AND PETIE
By Katharine Ross/Illustrated by Lisa McCue

UNDER THE MOON
By Joanne Ryder/Illustrated by Cheryl Harness

Just Right for 4's and 5's

THE CLEVER CARPENTER
By R. W. Alley

DOLLHOUSE MOUSE
By Natalie Standiford/Illustrated by Denise Fleming

PATRICK AND TED RIDE THE TRAIN
By Geoffrey Hayes

TIDY PIG
By Lucinda McQueen and Jeremy Guitar

Text copyright © 1988 by Arlene Blanchard. Illustrations copyright © 1988 by Vanessa Julian-Ottie. All rights reserved under International and Pan-American Copyright Conventions. Published in the United States by Random House, Inc., New York. Published in Great Britain by Methuen Children's Books, London. Created by Mathew Price Ltd., Old Rectory House, Marston Magna, Yeovil, Somerset BA22 8DT, England.

Library of Congress Cataloging-in-Publication Data: Blanchard, Arlene. Sounds my feet make. (A Just right book) SUMMARY: A child's feet make a variety of sounds walking in a puddle, stepping on a metal grid, trudging upstairs, and wearing different types of shoes. [1. Sound–Fiction. 2. Foot–Fiction] I. Julian-Ottie, Vanessa, ill. II. Title. III. Series: Just right book (New York, N.Y.) PZ7.B592So 1988 [E] 87-61699 ISBN: 0-394-89648-3

Manufactured in Singapore 1 2 3 4 5 6 7 8 9 0

JUST RIGHT BOOKS is a trademark of Random House, Inc.

A Just Right Book

SOUNDS
MY FEET MAKE

By Arlene Blanchard
Illustrated by Vanessa Julian-Ottie

Random House 🏠 New York

My feet go
splish! splash! splosh!
in the puddles on the way to Grandma's house.

My feet go

(((**clang!** (((**clang!** (((**clang!**

on the metal grid by the playground.

They go

swoosh! **swoosh!** **swoosh!**

through the dead leaves in my backyard.

And

squeak! **squeak!** **squeak!**

in my new shoes, which I *don't* like.

My feet go

THUMP!
THUMP!
THUMP!

up the stairs to my bath.

And

kersplash! kersplish!

in the bathtub before Mommy yells,
"Stop that splashing!"

But my feet can go quietly, too.
They go

shshshuffleshuffleshuffle

across the floor in my old yellow slippers.

And

tippytoe,   tippytoe,   tippytoe,

so quietly you can hardly hear them when
I creep into bed with Mommy and Daddy.

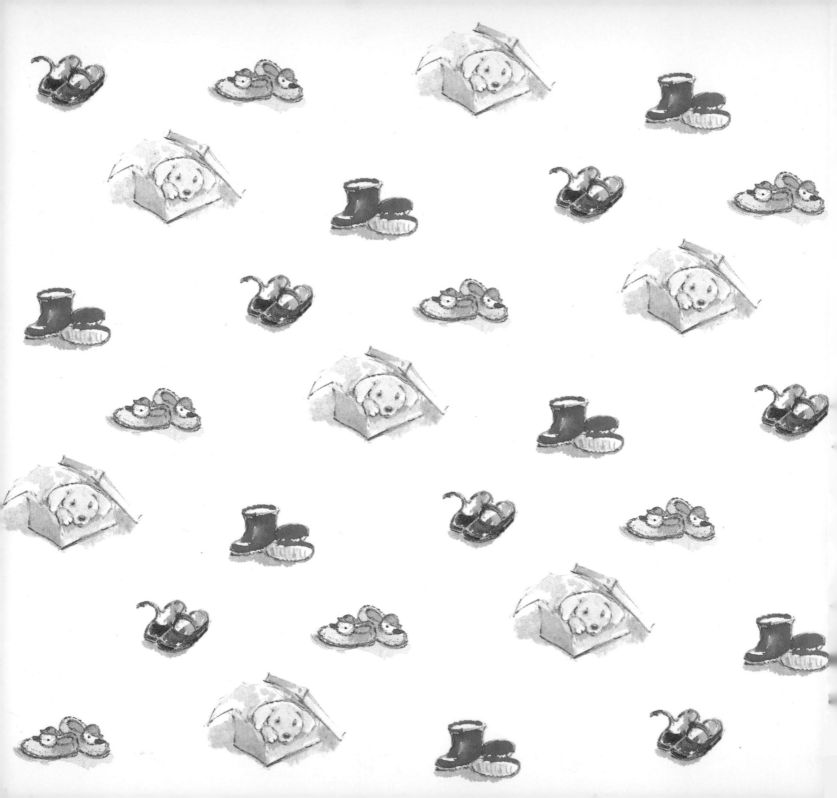